Last Call

and Other Short Fiction
by
Kaye Lynne Booth

Table of Contents

Newsletter

Want to keep up with all the latest on *WordCrafter*, *Writing to be Read*, and author Kaye Lynne Booth? Sign up for the monthly Kaye Lynne Booth email newsletter:
https://mailchi.mp/64aa2261e702/klb-wc-newsletter
Visit the *WordCrafter* website and social media pages:
Website: https://kayebooth.wixsite.com/wordcrafter
Facebook: https://www.facebook.com/WordCrafterServices/
LinkedIn: https://www.linkedin.com/company/
wordcrafter-enterprises/?viewAsMember=true

Last Call

I knew deep down that I shouldn't let Vicky get to me. It was just one more battle I was letting her win, even if it was a small one. It was just what she wanted. She was the root of my current predicament. She was the reason I was driving down this endless highway, through the barren wastelands of the desert with no clear destination in mind. Because of her, everything I owned was in the back of my truck.

Vicky was a bitch. There was no other way to describe her. Her favorite pass-time was to cause scenes in front of the customers where I worked. She thought it was funny. That ended when one customer left the store in disgust, after I had spent forty-five minutes convincing her to buy an expensive refrigerator. Who could blame my boss for firing me?

Actually, losing my job hadn't bothered me as much as you might think. I'd been a salesman for four years. I wasn't exactly climbing the corporate ladder. Suits and ties are not my thing. I'm not built to be a lumberjack, but my musculature is not what one would call lacking. I always looked like I was trying to pop out of the suits I wore to work. My hands are the calloused hands of a working man, the hands of a man who grew up on a farm, further proof that I'm no salesman. No, the loss of my job didn't stir much grief inside of me.

Being kicked out of my apartment, on the other hand, had bothered me a great deal. That's where Vicky started showing up after I lost my job. There was a time when Vicky had been a loving woman. Somewhere along the way she'd turned mean. Now all she ever wanted to do was fight.

She'd appear at my door, unannounced and uninvited; arguing, throwing things. Once, she jumped on top of me, pummeling me with her fists. The police said there was nothing that they could do. She'd left no marks. The cops didn't have a whole lot of empathy for me. They treated it as more of a joke. I guess it was kind of funny to picture little Vicky, who weighed all of ninety-five pounds, physically assaulting a big old lummox like me. She knew I wouldn't hit her back.

The last time the police showed up at my door, my landlord evicted me; she ran a respectable place, after all. I'd just gone out and sold my nine millimeter in order to pay the next month's rent, but she didn't want my money. She wanted me out.

So here I was, driving down this godforsaken highway, stretching out straight ahead for as far as I could see. I wasn't even sure where I was. I'd seen nothing but dried up sagebrush and cactus since morning. I had no idea where I was going. There was no one to care where I ended up.

The only reason I had for not to just ending it all was that I no longer had my gun. A gun was the only method that would be quick and painless. Maybe I'm a wimp, but I am not one to prolong suffering, least of all, my own.

No. That avenue was closed for now. I'd just wallow in my own misery, until I could figure out what I wanted to do with my life. Some people might look upon this as a chance for a new start, but to me, it felt more like the end.

The sun's rays beat down on my un-air-conditioned truck all day in the dry heat. It was so hot, even my sweat was no help cooling me off. The wind blowing in through the windows was hot and dry, doing little to ease my discomfort. Wherever I was, it was a far cry from civilization.

Ahead in the distance a building appeared on the horizon, breaking the monotony of the dried out sagebrush and endless sand. Maybe it was a mirage that would waver and fade as I approached it, but it didn't. As I got closer it solidified into a reality, a small wooden building with on windows, and a thick wooden door.

"What is this?" I wondered out loud to the empty cab. Only the hot wind answered.

There were a couple of cars in the parking lot, which spread out beneath a wooden sign. As I came closer, the words proclaiming this place "Last Call Tavern" became clear.

"Okay," I said to myself, "who would put a bar way out here in the middle of nowhere?" It didn't make any sense. Who would come all the way out here for a beer?

The heat was really getting to me. The temperature inside the cab must have been over one hundred. My sweat plastered the shirt to my back, even with both windows down. I could see waves of heat radiating off the pavement in front of me and my tongue stuck to the back of my throat.

The closer I got to the mysterious bar in the middle of nowhere, the better the idea of belting down a cold one sounded. I was pulling into the parking lot before I was even conscious of having decided to stop. I parked my paint worn Chevy pick-up next to a blue compact that was sitting below and to the right of the sign. Across the small lot, there was also a newer, double cab Ford pick-up, waiting for its owner to return from slaking his thirst.

I was planning on throwing back a couple of suds and maybe even grabbing a bite to eat, if they had a grill. I locked my doors and tightened the straps down on the tarp that was covering my load. That tarp was hot enough to fry an egg on.

I'd been traveling through the heat and glare of this desert all day and my throat felt like sandpaper. The cold beer was fast becoming a priority for me. By the time I pulled open the heavy wooden door, I could think of little else.

The inside of the building was covered with dark, rich paneling. The dim lighting of the neon bar signs was a sharp contrast to the brightness of the glaring desert sunlight, so it took a couple of minutes for my eyes to adjust. There were two people, sitting in the shadows in the corner booth; undoubtedly the owners of the two cars outside. In the dim lighting, all I could make out was that they were man and woman. It made the room feel heavy and sad.

"Some Beach" by Blake Shelton was playing on the jukebox, adding to my hopeless attitude. There were no beaches in store for me. My head began a low throb that promised to become a slow rumba. I strode across the room to the dark mahogany bar, where a stout, muscular bartender was dressed in black jeans and a black silk shirt. Hair tied back in a ponytail, he smiled and ask for my order.

"Give me a beer. Whatever you have on tap is fine."

"Yes, Sir," the barkeep replied. "Just pull up that barstool. We've been expecting you." He nodded his head toward the leather covered bar stool to my right.

It took a couple of seconds for his words to sink in. "What do you mean by that?"

I was talking to myself. The bartender was already down at the end of the bar drawing the golden liquid into the tipped, frosted glass. I shrugged, pulling up the barstool, I slid my formidable frame onto the brown rawhide seat.

Flash!!!

Lightning struck within the bar. My mind could find no other explanation for the blinding flash of light that seared through the room. Instinctively, I threw my arms up, covering my eyes.

I rubbed my eyes to help them adjust again, but the dimly lit bar had been replaced by the scorching desert sunlight, glaring at me through windows that had not been there, only moments ago. The rich mahogany of the bar had also been replaced by a shiny clean Formica countertop with little silver speckles throughout. "What the...?"

"Here you are, friend." said the bartender, smiling as he slid the frosty cold mug in front of me. It was the same guy, but now he was dressed all in white, an ice cream stained apron around his waist, and his ponytail had transformed into a buzz cut.

The smooth golden liquid had been replaced as well. What sat in front of me was a dark and foamy liquid, with the pungent aroma of root beer. A mound of ice cream peeked out at me from the depths of the glass.

"I ordered a beer," I didn't know what was happening, but my throat was parched and I'd been looking forward to that beer.

"Root beer float, Sir," he replied, smiling. "Just as you ordered."

"No, I ordered a damn beer! That's what I ordered!" I slammed my fist down on the counter top that was no longer a bar. A mighty thirst had risen within me and a root beer float wasn't going to cut it. "Cut the crap and draw me a..."

I froze, taking in more of my surroundings. There was a milkshake machine where the tap had been a moment ago and across from that, at the end of the counter, was a freezer unit with a glass top, so customers could look inside and choose their flavor.

"What the hell is going on here?"

"Sir?" the man behind the counter questioned.

"Aw, come on," I said, "don't pretend like you don't know what I'm talking about. Didn't you just see me walk in here when it was dark? There were no windows, and this... this counter was a mahogany bar. Remember, you had a ponytail and I ordered a beer, but you brought me this ice cream crap for little kids instead." I swept my arm across the counter, sending the root beer float crashing to the floor on the other side.

"That's all right, Sir," the bartender said with a slight smile on his face. "I'll have that cleaned up in a jiffy. Can I get you another one? Folks say that my root beer floats make life worth living."

I sounded crazy, even to my own ears. There was no question I was losing it, panic rising. "I need to get outta here," I said, sliding down from the stool I'd been perched on. It now had a red seat and sported a wrought iron back.

The bartender, or whatever he was, just nodded knowingly, smiling as if people came in here and rambled off stuff that didn't make any sense every day. "Are you sure that you won't have that root beer float before you go, Sir?"

This was just too weird. It had the feeling of an episode in *The Twilight Zone*. I shoved my stool back from the counter hard, almost falling over backwards as I did.

"No, I don't want a root beer float!" I exclaimed, shaking my head in disbelief. "Can't you hear? I need to get outta here!"

As I picked myself up and headed for the door, my eyes swept the room. A family, with a young boy and a teenaged girl replaced the couple in the corner booth, and two gentlemen played checkers at a table by the windows, next to the juke box. All eyes rested on me. There was a series of clicks as a record dropped in the silence, then Doris Day began singing, "A Chocolate Sundae on a Saturday Night" from the jukebox. I recognized the song because it was a song my mother had played all the time when I was a kid.

A young woman, wearing a white blouse with a pleated, sky-blue skirt, bobby socks and Penny Loafers cleaned a nearby table. She wore her hair in a pony tail that bobbed back and forth as she rubbed her cleaning cloth over the Formica tabletop, and she smacked her gum loudly. Or at least, she had been smacking her gum until the crazy guy that was me had come in, raising a fuss about how stuff was different than it had been a few minutes ago. Now she silently stared at me, like everyone else. I knew what it felt like to be a bug under a microscope.

"What just happened?" I screamed at them. No one responded, but eyes widened as my voice rose.

I backed into the, now glass, door. I reached back and pushed it open, jingling the bells attached to announce arrivals and departures. I backed out into the parking lot, not taking my eyes off of the people through the windows, who were all still staring back at me in wonder, or puzzlement.

As I turned and headed towards the spot where I had parked my truck, I stopped dead in my tracks. Even the parking lot had changed. There were three cars now, all older models, from the nineteen-fifties or sixties. A black coupe of unknown make and model that resembled an upside-down bathtub on wheels sat where my truck had been. My truck and everything I owned was gone.

I gazed up at the sign above me, which was no longer the faded wooden one that I had seen in front of the tavern when I pulled in. Now, in large, bright red letters on a plain white, plastic background, it proclaimed the place, "Sundaes Soda Shoppe: Where Every Day is Sundae".

The only things that hadn't changed were the long, straight stretch of highway and the surrounding landscape, barren of all vegetation except sagebrush and cactus. A small lime green lizard skittered across the pavement in front of me. No home, no job - now, no life. "Now what do I do?" I asked the hot, dry air, as I scanned my surroundings.

I was sitting in the middle of a nowhere that was not where it was a few minutes ago. It sounded crazy, but the only other possibility was that I was losing my mind. Then again, that was probably the case. After all, I was standing in a blazing hot parking lot, staring into the desert sun and talking to myself. Crazy or not, I had absolutely nothing left, nowhere to go and no way to get there. My legs grew weak and wobbly. I crumpled to my butt in the middle of the parking lot. Hot, wet tears streamed down my face, their salty taste stinging my lips. How could things get any worse?

Not even Vicky, with all the arguments and hassles, had been able to reduce me to a blubbering idiot, sitting in the middle of a hot parking lot, burning my butt off on the sizzling pavement, bawling my fricking eyes out. I thought she'd won, but now I realized that her little victories had all been minor. Now, looking at the black boat sitting in the spot where my truck should have been, I realized that it was actually possible for me to sink even further into despair.

The sound of an engine, racing up the highway brought me back to the here and now, wherever and whenever that was. My butt felt like a half roasted chicken and I needed to move it before it was fully cooked. I wiped my face with my shirt sleeve and got to my feet. I couldn't very well walk out of there, and I didn't want to stand out in the blazing parking lot to fry. The only thing left to do was to turn around and go back into the bar, or the Soda Shoppe, or whatever it was.

As I reached for the glass door, the car I'd heard came sliding into the parking lot, sending up a spray of gravel. When it came to a stop, I could see it was a '53 Corvette, powder blue and white, with a blonde beauty, wearing dark glasses, at the wheel. I know what year it was, because I'm a Corvette connoisseur. I'm crazy about them, and now that I'd thought about it, I'm rather fond of attractive blondes, as well. After I'd given the car and the girl the once over, not wanting to stare, I pulled open the door and went back inside, the tinkling bells announcing my arrival.

The man behind the counter smiled when he saw me enter. "You decided to have that root beer float after all." he said.

"No." I replied, "I just needed to come in here to figure things out. What else do you have?"

"We have soda and we have several flavors of ice cream," said the counter guy, "but my root beer floats are really the best."

"All right, fine," I conceded. "Make me a root beer float." I pulled up a chair at the table closest to the door and sat down. "Can you bring it over here though? I'm still a little shaky."

"Indeed I can, Sir," he said, with a smile. There was a joyful bounce in his step as he went to make it. I hadn't realized that my drinking a lousy root beer float would make the guy so happy.

Tony Bennett was singing about a "Stranger in Paradise", as the family in the corner booth got up to leave, eying me warily. I felt like a stranger here, but I wasn't sure that this was paradise.

"Mommy, what's wrong with that man?" a little blonde girl of about six or seven asked. She wore a pretty pink dress and black patent-leather shoes, and her hair was done up in two pigtails that were slightly uneven.

"Nothing, honey," her mother replied, with a touch of her finger tips to her bouffant hair-do. "He's probably been out in the sun too long."

The father came up behind mother and daughter, ushering them out the door with haste, but the boy, who was about twelve, stopped to stare at me. "Jimmy, come along," the father said. "You know staring is not polite."

"Coming, Dad," the boy in the stripped shirt and blue jeans said, rushing to catch up with his family.

The girl with the bobby socks brought my root beer float, pony tail swinging from side to side, and set it down on the table in front of me. I smiled at her and said, "Thanks."

She blew a bubble as she trotted back toward the counter and the bells tinkled above the door as the family exited.

Realizing just how thirsty I really was from being out in the heat, I reached over and brought the mug to my lips. The cold, creamy ice cream combined with the fizzy pungent taste of the root beer was absolutely divine. I hadn't known that anything could taste this good. After just one sip, I thought that I was feeling the best I'd felt over the span of the entire past year.

As I set the mug back on the table, the bells tinkled above the door once more as the blonde from the Vette walked in. She took off her sunglasses to reveal the most beautiful green eyes that I had ever seen. They were such a brilliant, clear shade of green, that they could have been shining emeralds. She returned my stare until I felt uncomfortable enough to look away and take another sip of my float. She didn't let it drop there, though. She walked straight over to my table and asked, "Mind if I join you?"

I looked up at her, "Please. Help yourself." I spread my arm in the direction of the seat across the table. She pulled the chair that I had indicated over next to my own and took a seat.

"Hi, my name is Christine," she said, "but people call me Chrissy."

"Nice to meet you, Chrissy," I replied. "I'm Luke." I felt a connection with this woman that was beyond my ability to explain. Her golden hair splayed out across the champagne pink shoulders of her silk blouse, and her blue pleated skirt came down to just above her knees, topping off a pair of the shapeliest legs that I had ever seen.

"I saw you when I pulled in." she said, "I figured that you had to be here for a root beer float."

"Yeah, nice car. '53 right?" I asked.

"Brand new, right off the lot, just last week." she replied.

I choked on my float, trying not to spit it all over this gorgeous woman who had chosen to strike up a conversation with me. When I had myself under control once again, I questioned her further. "Did you say it's a brand new '53?"

"Yep. That's what I said." she replied, nodding and smiling, "Is there something the matter with that?"

Things were suddenly falling into place for me, at least, in a manner of speaking. The cars, the fashions, even the Soda Shoppe all cried out 1950's. Somehow, I had traveled back in time. For some reason, I felt as if this woman held the key to figuring it all out.

"Why did you think that I came for a root beer float?" I wondered.

"Well, didn't you?" she responded, smiling and pointing to the mug in front of me.

"No, actually I..." I stopped in mid-sentence, as I looked down and realized that my mug was empty. I had sat there and drank the whole thing, without even knowing it. I realized something else, too. I was smiling. I'd been so miserable over the past year, that I couldn't remember the last time that I had smiled. "...well, yeah, actually I guess that I did. I just didn't know it," I said in amazement. "Would you like one? They really are very good."

"No, thank you," she said. "I had one once.

That was a rather strange response, but then this had been a rather strange day. "So, you can't have another?" I asked, widening my smile.

"Don't need another one," she replied. "One will last for a lifetime."

I thought about her words, pondering their meaning. Then, I thought about how I was feeling. I felt good. I felt happy, just sitting here, talking with this woman. I felt better than I had in a very long time. I felt like... like, life was worth living again. "So, it never goes away?" I asked Chrissy.

She didn't ask what I meant. She just said, "Nope. It stays with you, whether you stay or go back."

"What do you mean go back? You can go back?"

She nodded. "If you really want to. All you have to do is hop back up onto the stool there at the soda fountain." She pointed to the very same stool I'd been sitting on earlier. "Or..." she said, "you could come and jump into my car with me instead. You and I could travel places."

"As tempting as that sounds," I told her, "I don't think I really belong here." I wasn't sure what was going on. Maybe I had a bad case of heat stroke, or maybe I'd gone off the deep end, but I knew this wasn't reality. Or at least, it wasn't my reality.

"Are you sure?" Chrissy asked. "I don't make that offer to every guy that makes his way up onto that stool."

"No, I think I'd better try and put things back to normal," I said rising from the table with a shake of my head.

"Suit yourself," she replied with a shrug of her shoulders, "but we could have fun."

"Thanks just the same," I said, walking back over to the stool. "I think I should go back."

I turned and looked back at Chrissy. She smiled and wiggled her fingers at me in a light hearted farewell. I pulled the stool out and slid up onto it.

FLASH!!!

This time when I opened my eyes, I was back in the dark tavern, a mug of cold beer sitting on the bar in front of me. The jukebox was blaring "There's Got to be Something More" by Sugarland. I picked the mug in front of me, intending to chug back the long awaited beer, but I stopped, holding the frothy brew in mid-air between the bar and my lips. I wasn't thirsty anymore. I set the mug back on the bar and slid down off of the stool.

Digging a couple of bills from my jean pocket and throwing them onto the bar, I headed across the room and pushed open the heavy oak door. Outside once again, my pick-up was sitting right where I had left it, with all of my meager belongings packed into the back.

Gazing over the tarp that covered all I owned in the world, I realized what I'd told Chrissy wasn't quite true. It was here that I no longer felt I belonged. I had no home, no job, no one to come home to. I couldn't think of one thing that was keeping me here, but realizing that, it somehow didn't seem so depressing to admit it anymore.

I made a split second decision. I took my keys out of my pocket, tossing them on top of the tarp covering what was left of my life. Smiling once more, I turned around and went back into the Last Call Tavern, but for me it wasn't the last call anymore.

I went through the solid door and marched across the floor, this time with purpose. I jumped back up onto the stool. From now on, for me, every day was Sundae.

Terror on the Mountain Trail

It was a warm spring day when Randy and I set out up the trail. Randy rode his Honda dirt bike. I followed on my Kawasaki Bayou. The ATV was packed with the makings for a lovely picnic: chicken salad sandwiches, trail mix, plums and a six pack of pop. It was a beautiful day in late April.

The trail was not an easy one, but we had ridden it countless times before and I traversed it with little difficulty. In fact, this was one of my favorite trails for that very reason. It wasn't too steep or too rocky, yet it still presented several challenging stretches. Though there were rough spots and places where it thinned, tilting to one side and making it necessary to lean to the up-side of the hill to stay balanced, I rode the trail with confidence.

It took us about an hour to reach the spot where we had planned to lunch. Randy could have reached it in half the time on his bike, but I was slower on the Bayou. Randy usually rode on ahead, then circled back so I wasn't left behind. Randy always did little things like that. He looked out for me.

The area was a flat grassy area with wild flowers sprinkled throughout. Randy took great care not to smash any of the wild flowers that spotted the open field in purples and yellows, as he spread the blanket out. He knew how much I loved them. I've always been nature's daughter, considering the flora and fauna to be my kin. I loved him for the care he took in avoiding the delicate blooms.

Randy chuckled as he watched me unpack the cooler with care, setting everything just right. If the blanket had been red and white plaid instead of the soft sky blue, it could have been a scene right out of a storybook, one with a happy ending.

The funny thing was, I knew he was watching me as I laid out our picnic, and I took my time setting each item out on the blanket with exaggerated care. I was well aware of how much the view of my butt in tight denim turned him on, and I used every opportunity I saw to show it off properly. I had high hopes of a little afternoon romp in the woods. After twenty years of marriage, I knew a lot of little things about Randy and I used them to my advantage. Randy took notice every time I bent over. He always noticed.

We casually enjoyed their lunch, then lay back watching the clouds float lazily across the sky's blue expanse, talking of things we hoped the future would have in store.

"We should take another trip to Mesa Verde next summer, before the boys get too old," he said. "Marty will be in high school next year."

"So?" I said. "Is there some sudden magical age when teenage boys are all of the sudden too old to go on family vacations?"

"No, but before you know it, his whole world will become girls and cars," Randy said. "Hanging out with his friends will be much more appealing than going on vacation with his parents."

"It won't be long until they're both grown and gone you know," I said.

"Yep, then it will be just you and me," he replied, leaning over to kiss my softly.

I kissed him back and before we knew it, it had turned into something more. We made love there on the blanket in the grass, with the sun beating down on them and the smell of pine penetrating each heavy breath we took. Afterwards, we both lay on the blanket with limbs entwined, trying to catch our breath.

Randy rolled over and looked at his watch.

"We'd better head back soon if we plan to be on time to pick up the kids," he said, reaching for his pants, which lay in a crumpled pile at the foot of the blanket.

I placed everything back in the cooler, while Randy loaded up the ATV, strapping it all down tight.

"Why don't you wear the nine-millimeter on your belt going down," he said, handing me his gun. "It bounced around a lot on the way up. The ATV will be a smoother ride for it."

I took it from him and secured it on my belt. We were ready to ride.

I rode down at my own speed. Randy rode out front a ways, leisurely looping back to putt along with me for a while before he sped ahead once more. He never got too far ahead of me. I knew if I had any problems, it wouldn't be long before he came back to give me a hand. I took my time, enjoying the beautiful mountain scenery with no worries.

I loved to ride with Randy because he was so attentive; always making sure that I'm doing okay, sometimes stopping to wait, after more difficult stretches of trail just to make sure I could do it. If we did come to something which I felt was too hard, he would take the driver's seat and get me over it.

Today was no different. Randy rode up ahead, and I was riding along, thinking that we might have time to stop and buy a cold drink before picking up the kids. The heat of the day had pretty much diminished the ice in the cooler and the rest of the pop we had with us was pretty warm, even before we started down.

From the corner of my eye, I caught a glimpse of blue through the trees ahead. I stopped my vehicle, as I always did, to give hikers the right of way. But, when I got a good view of the man coming up the trail, alarm bells began to go off in my head. Something wasn't right.

The man looked rather scraggly, with his dirty blonde hair hanging down in his face and he was wearing a blue down jacket in the smoldering heat. His eyes were wide and glassy, and he carried a huge rock, three times the size of his hand. He looked higher than a kite, or like a junky in need of a fix.

My mind began to race. Where was Randy? He should be circling back by now. Had this guy been hiding off the trail when he went by? I know my husband, and if Randy had seen this weird guy, he would have hightailed it back here. The thought of being up here alone with this weirdo and Randy not knowing gave me the creeps. It was possible though. We were almost down. Maybe Randy hadn't seen this guy. Maybe he'd decided to head to the car and start loading.

It was up to me. I had to do something. If I tried to go forward, I'd run head on into the guy. He staggered right up the middle of the trail, leaving no room on either side to go around. I pulled in the clutch and stepped down on the shifter. There was a trick to getting the Bayou into reverse, and I always had difficulty with it. Now, I was overcome with urgency, almost on the verge of panic, and my machine refused to be forced.

I looked up. The guy was gaining ground, but everything seemed to happen in slow motion. I spotted Randy over the guy's shoulder. He was scrambling to his feet, crab-walking on all fours up the hill. Where was his bike? Randy must have encountered this guy further down the mountain. The guy probably thought Randy was down for the count. I didn't call out, because I had an idea that whatever was happening here, we needed the element of surprise.

I tried to throw the ATV into reverse again, but still couldn't find the gear. All I could do was sit there as the crazy guy with the rock came closer. He was only about two feet away from me now. I found myself downwind from a brown bear once while hiking in the mountains, almost gagging from his odor. The stench of the man's body odor was more repugnant, even at that distance.

I looked over his shoulder to check on Randy's progress as I tried to hit reverse again. Randy was up on his feet now, but he was still quite a ways down the trail. Randy's progress up the hill seemed to be in slow motion along with everything else. I didn't see how he could possibly reach me in time, and apparently, neither did Randy.

"Kellie, get the gun!" he yelled, reaching down to pick up a rock in each hand. "That guy's trying to kill us!"

So much for the element of surprise. Then it dawned on me. Randy was unarmed. I had the gun. Randy always carried a gun, especially in the mountains, where encounters with large predators were not uncommon. The realization that I was armed and he wasn't snapped me back to my senses.

The crazed man turned and looked back down the trail at Randy. The look of surprise on his face told me I'd been right about him being unaware of Randy. As my gloved hand fumbled to unsnap the holster on my belt, the rock fell from his hand and his eyes focused on the gun.

Before I knew it, his hand was on mine, trying to pry it off the gun. If he got a hold of the gun, we'd be finished. I slammed my other hand over his and squeezed, pressing down with all my might. His other hand came down over mine. For a moment that seemed like a lifetime I thought of the hand game I used to play with my grandfather, where the hand on the bottom pulls out and takes the top. I pictured myself pulling my bottom hand out from beneath the pile. A ridiculous idea under the circumstances, but I can't deny that it was there for a single fleeting moment. He threw his weight against me, lying across my lap, pinning me to the ATV beneath him as we struggled for the gun.

Randy stumbled, the rocks flying from his hands. He lunged, throwing himself onto the attacker, with one arm around the guy, the other, jerking the guy's top hand off of the pile.

Randy threw his weight into the guy, pressing him against my body to keep him from grabbing me again. As soon as he freed my hands, I fumbled with the holster and got it unsnapped.

"What the hell is going on?" I cried, as the two men wrestled in my lap, pinning my legs to the ATV.

"He's trying to kill us," Randy yelled. "Just get the gun."

"I got it!" I exclaimed, yanking the gun out of the holster.

I didn't realize it at the time, but Randy held the guy so his arms were pinned beneath him, so he couldn't wriggle free. With no other way to free himself, the guy turned his head and bit into the arm that held him.

"Cock it!" he yelled. "Hurry!"

As I held out the gun, my mind went blank as to how to cock it. I had shot this gun many times before, but suddenly I couldn't remember how to chamber the cartridge. This was all so surreal. A part of my mind kept insisting it couldn't be happening. The adrenaline rushed through my body. Instead of using the slide, I pulled back the hammer, like you would a revolver.

"No!" Randy exclaimed. He reached around the struggling man across my legs and took the gun from my hand. Somehow, he chambered the shell with only one hand, when I couldn't seem to do it with two.

Randy slammed the barrel up against the guy's temple. In that moment, I knew my husband was going to shoot the guy. At point blank range, there was no way he could miss. Fortunately, Randy was smart enough to realize I was on the other side of our opponent. I squeezed my eyes shut, waiting for the rapport, envisioning the bullet going right through the guy and into me, but the sound never came.

Instead, Randy grabbed a handful of down jacket with one hand and flung the guy out and away from us, throwing him over the edge of the trail. The guy went flying backwards down the hill, arms and legs splayed out in front of him, eyes wide with surprise, like something in a Superman comic. He landed on his back in a bush, about halfway down the steep embankment. I gave a sigh of relief that Randy hadn't shot him. I'd been sure that was the outcome we'd been headed for.

"Randy, he's still coming," I cried, unable to believe my own eyes, as the crazed man rose to his feet and staggered up the hill toward us, like a zombie who wouldn't die. He just kept coming.

Before I realized what was happening, Randy turned the gun on the guy and pulled the trigger. The man grunted, feathers from his down jacket floating out behind him, but still, he kept coming up the hill toward us. Randy moved his arm to the left and popped off two more shots.

I'd heard the shots ring out. I saw the guy's eyes grow wide as the feathers flew. I followed him with my eyes as he turned, running down the hill, unable to believe he was still standing. Randy had scared him off. Thank God. That was what was important.

"What do we do?" I asked. My heart was racing, pounding so hard that I thought it might pop right out of my chest.

"Take me to my bike," Randy replied.

The Bayou was still running. I threw it into gear as Randy threw his leg over behind me and we raced down to where his bike lay in the middle of the trail.

"Let me make sure my bike starts," he said, jumping off the ATV. "Then go as fast as you can, and don't stop until you get to the car."

"He went the other way," I said. "He can't catch us on bikes."

"What if he wasn't alone?" Randy yelled, picking up his bike.

Randy was like that, always thinking about the possibilities that would have never even crossed my mind. And this was one idea that truly had never occurred to me, but now that the idea had been placed in my mind. I couldn't help but think of the implications. Suddenly, the forest seemed menacing, with the possibility of danger behind every tree. A lump formed in the back of my throat as I glanced back up the trail. No more questions. I searched the trees ahead, scanning for movement, but all was still.

As Randy kick started his bike, I caught a glimpse of movement from the trail above. Maybe it was my imagination, picking up on the idea Randy had placed in my head, but I wasn't taking any chances.

"I think your right," I said. "Hurry!"

He started his bike and we were both off, flying down the trail. We were going faster than I'd ever taken that trail before, but I rode with determination and skill. When I looked back, Randy was right behind me.

He yelled for me to stop. I hit the brakes hard, sliding to a stop. He pulled up next to me. "I didn't kill him!" Randy exclaimed.

"I know you didn't. He ran off into the trees," I said, stating what I felt was obvious.

"Are you sure?" he asked.

"Yes," I said. "He left on his own two feet. Dead men don't run. Now can we get the hell off this mountain?"

"Okay," he said, sounding somewhat relieved. "Go! Go!"

We sped down the trail once again. It was good that I knew this trail as well as I did. Randy could ride anything with expert skill. He'd been riding all of his life. On the other hand, I had only been riding a short time and didn't have near his experience. At this speed, I only hoped I knew the trail well enough to make it down in one piece. I knew Randy wanted me to go faster because he was almost on top of me, but I didn't want to crash on this trail with that guy still running loose.

Randy yelled for me to stop again. I hit the brakes. What was it now? We had to get out of here. Randy pulled up next to my once again.

"We have to call the cops," he said. I wasn't sure if it was a statement or a question.

"Okay," I said, "Let's get down to where we can get a signal on the cell. Come on." I didn't know why he was wasting time like this. We were almost to the car.

"Wait. I didn't kill him, did I?" he said in a shaky voice. He sounded almost frantic.

"Randy, he ran off!" I exclaimed. "What do you think?"

"But I shot him," Randy snapped back. "What if he just ran until he bled out? What if he's laying up there dead?"

"To hell with that, Randy!" I almost spat the words at him. "We could have been lying up there dead! He tried to kill us!"

"No, wait," he said. "What if he's not dead? What if I didn't even hit him, but just scared him? What if he attacks someone else? We have to tell the police, so they can try to catch him."

I thought about this for a second. "You're right," I said. "I wouldn't want anyone else to be hurt. He was trying to kill us, for God's sake. I'll report it as soon as we get to the truck. It'll be okay...." I was rambling now, losing it on the trail. This wasn't good. We had to make it off this mountain. Then I could fall apart if I had to.

"Hey, stop Kellie," he said. "It'll be okay. Let's just get back down to the truck. Then we'll decide what to do."

When we reached the end of the trail, Randy quickly loaded the bike and ATV onto the trailer. I stood watch, scanning the trail and the surrounding shrubbery, half expecting the crazy guy, or maybe a friend he'd brought along, to appear out of nowhere. There was no way that he could have made it to the parking area as fast as we had, even if Randy hadn't put a bullet in him, but I watched, just the same.

Randy strapped both vehicles into the trailer securely. We both jumped into the truck. As soon as we were headed down the road, I started trying to get a signal. I called the police, arranging to meet an officer at a nearby gas station. Then, I called the school to tell them we'd be delayed in picking up the boys.

The officer arrived and we gave our report, showing him the dent in Randy's helmet from the impact of the rock. The officer took our report and we returned to the scene to show the police exactly where it happened.

The police never did find the crazy guy with the rock. I watched the papers for some time after that, noting any reports of missing persons in that area. There were several. A young man who set out on a day hike and was never seen again. A couple of teen girls who disappeared from the neighborhood below the trail. Nothing that might be connected, unless you were looking for it. When I read reports, I had to wonder. He could still up there somewhere, preying on unsuspecting hikers.

Earth Mother

All was dark. So, the creator, who we call Earth Mother, took heat from her essence and focused it into a ball and spit it out into a blazing orb in the vast expanse. This was not an easy task, and she choked on it several times before it was finally emitted. Her coughing spasms caused hot spittle to fly across the expanse, sprinkling it with billions of tiny sparkling orbs from one end to the other.

Earth Mother was pleased by the sparkling expanse that she had created, but she soon grew bored looking at all the shining orbs that filled the expanse with twinkling light. She decided there had to be more, so she scraped off some skin into her hand and blew the flakes over the surface of a large boiling spit ball, creating land amid the water.

It was pleasing to her, this cooling ball of skin and spit, but soon she grew bored once more. So, Earth Mother cut off her hair, her most treasured feature, into tiny pieces and sprinkled it over the earth. Then she breathed life into each little piece of hair with one breath from within her.

But they were all alike, so Earth Mother was not pleased with the hair creatures that she had created. She buried some of the hair creatures, both large and small, in the ground and they sprang forth in beautiful shades of green and brown. Some of them spurted forth flower heads and produced seeds that were carried forth on the winds of Earth Mother's breath.

Then Earth Mother took her fingernail and sliced several slit-like gashes on the faces of the hair creatures that had landed in the waters of her saliva, allowing them to breathe. She shaped the hair creatures that had landed on her flesh into various shapes to differentiate them. Some, she gave four legs fashioned from the flesh of her own legs, so they could run very fast over the earth's skin. Some, she gave wings, fashioned from the essence of her own wings, so that they could fly above the earth. To the tiniest creatures, she gave many tiny legs, at least six, sometimes more. She shook out some dander from her wings, but there were a lot of tiny creatures and she was easily distracted, so only some of the tiny creatures could take to the air. She fashioned some hair creatures into long stringy ropes, which could slide along the earth's skin, and to some water creatures, she gave legs, allowing them to live either on the skin or in the spittle. She used black pigment from her hair, brown pigment from her skin, green and blue pigment from her eyes, yellow pigment from her urine, white pigment from her fingernails and red pigment from her blood to decorate them, making each species of creature unique.

These newly fashioned creatures roamed the earth, and Earth Mother was pleased, but soon she once again became bored. So, she took some left-over bits of hair, added some flesh from her legs to give them each two legs. She wanted these creatures to be interesting, so she cut into her head and removed a large chunk. This she crushed into a fine powder, which she blew over the two-legged creatures, so they could think and reason and be motivated to something besides wandering about, procreating, like all of the other creatures she had created. While she was spreading the dust from her head, some went up her nose and made her sneeze, so not all of the two-legged creatures got an equal share, but for the most part, it worked. Now the Earth Mother could sit back and watch these creatures and be truly entertained. And that is just what she did.

A Turn of the Tables

The sign on the door read Melina Dupree, M.D. - Psychiatrist. Michael straightened his lapel on his pinstriped suit, focusing on creating a mental shield before entering the office. Without it, mortals often felt ill at ease around his kind. The Elder Council wanted him to keep a low profile and had warned Michael to control his temper when he was chosen for the assignment. The council needed this mortal alive for now. Her research on how blood pathogens affect certain brain disorders had yielded information that could be quite unsettling to the entire vampire society.

Dr. Dupree had not found what she was looking for, but unwittingly, one of the pathogens she'd created had the potential to wipe out all vampires. It was unknown whether she herself, realized what her research had uncovered. Under other circumstances the Elder Council would have the research destroyed and she would be eliminated. But this mortal was surrounded by the aura of a coven of powerful witches, sworn enemies of all vampires. Her connection to the Sarenrea wasn't clear, but Michael's instructions were to bring her before the council without alerting the coven.

He pushed open the glass door to the office. Two large salt water fish tanks almost covered an entire wall on either side of the waiting room. Six tacky leather chairs sat in line in front of a gray metal desk. A girl, perhaps in her early twenties, with straight blond hair and too much make-up, sat behind the desk filing her nails. She looked up as he entered.

"Please tell Dr. Dupree that Michael Wymond is here to see her," he said, meeting her gaze with an intense stare.

The girl sat up straighter, scanning her appointment book. She pushed the button on the intercom on her desk. "Dr. Dupree, your seven o'clock appointment is here."

Michael's gaze did not waver from the girl behind the desk. It wouldn't do for her to be here when he took Dupree out.

"Send him in."

The girl looked up, meeting his gaze before glancing away to stare at the intercom with a blank expression. Without saying a word, she reached under the desk, grabbing her purse and sweater, and left the office. Michael smiled at the thought of her hitting the street, realizing she had no idea where she was headed.

In the inner office, the antique furnishings appeared authentic. They included a wooden filing cabinet next to a free-standing mirror to his left, a beveled glass bookshelf lining the right wall, a Victorian-style Chaise lounge that no doubt served as the "analysis couch" next to the wall, and the oak desk, which Dr. Dupree sat behind.

The Sarenrae aura hit Michael strong, as the doctor peered over her black-framed librarian's glasses at him, smiling. He wondered if she chose that style to make her look more intellectual. It was a look that worked, combined with her sandy blond hair pulled back in a ponytail, and her blue tailored skirt and blazer. She was the perfect picture of what a psychiatrist should be, albeit a sexy one.

Her female scent was sensual. This one had pheromones dripping off her. It stirred the maleness left within him, hardening his member as if he were still mortal. He detected the odor of fresh sex emanating from between her thighs. She'd been fucked not long ago, and still the scent of her need clung to her.

He closed his eyes, blocking his mind to those sexual thoughts, which he knew could lead nowhere. At the same time, he opened himself to her mind to see what he might learn. It was strange that he sensed no malice from her. A Sarenrae should be able to detect his true nature even with his mind shielded, but she seemed to be unaware.

When he opened his eyes, she was checking him out. Her eyes roved up and down him as she accessed the muscular man standing before her in a dark blue hoodie and black jeans. "How may I help you, Mr. Wymond?" she asked, tipping her head just a fraction to the side, her deep violet-blue eyes penetrating the depths of his stare.

Such strange eyes, meeting his gaze and holding it, drawing his eyes to hers. He'd play it cool while he probed her mind more for the answers he sought.

"I'm not here as a patient," he said.

Her aura was strong and unmistakable, but he sensed no conscious connection with the coven. Then, a shield snapped up around her mind, like a light bulb burning out, and her thoughts were closed to him. It caught him off guard. Most mortals didn't have strong enough minds to keep him out, but this one didn't even seem to be aware that she'd done it.

She gazed at him with raised brow. "Then why are you here?"

With her mind shielded, subtle was out. He chose a more direct approach. "I'm a vampire," he said with a smile, taking a seat on the leather armchair across the desk from her.

"A vampire?" She peered over her glasses at him once more, the corners of her mouth turning up ever so slightly, her brows raised over those deep blue eyes. "Of course. Is that why you request an evening appointment?" she asked.

Michael ran his hand up over the top of his head, pushing unruly black curls back from his face. Her disbelief seemed genuine. He took a deep breath, reminding himself to have patience with this mortal. He needed her, for now. "You think I'm crazy," he said, placing his hands on the desk across from her. "You should be quaking with fear, but you're not."

She looked up, again meeting his gaze. "Those in my profession prefer not to label people in such manner," she said, scribbling something on the yellow legal pad in front of her.

Each time she tipped her head as she wrote he could see her jugular pulsing in her beautifully curved neck. That, combined with the smell of her blood created a strong urge in him to jump over the desk and drink her dry, but he knew he couldn't risk it. Perhaps when the Elder Council had finished with her...

"So, you wish to be feared?" she asked, with a smirk on her face and a gleam in her eye.

She was analyzing him. Mortals had always played mind games throughout the centuries, trying to get the best of one another. He took a seat on the "analysis couch". He would beat her at her own game. He leaned back, swinging his legs up into the "good patient" position. "Of course, I want to be feared," he said. "I'm a vampire. But you don't fear me."

She shook her head. "Why do you think that is?" she asked, peeking over her glasses at him once more.

"You don't believe," Michael said, staring up at the ceiling, "but I don't understand why. You should believe, even if you're not afraid." He knew all she saw was a well-dressed young man in his early twenties, claiming to be a vampire. If she was Sarenae, her attitude didn't make sense. "Perhaps I was mistaken in coming here."

"I don't think you were mistaken," she said, the corners of her mouth inching up just the slightest fraction. It felt as if those violet-blue eyes penetrated down to the depths of his soul, as if he had one. "You've promised to make my evening interesting. Tell me, why did you come here, Michael?"

He turned to face her. She had eyes the color of morning glories opening to the dawn. It had been centuries since Michael had witnessed the sun rising. That was one of the few things he missed about mortal life, the beauty of the morning sun, rising to wake the earth and all her children. But, he didn't come here to admire her eyes.

"Your research on blood pathogens," he said, breaking away from her gaze.

She set down her pencil. The trace of a smile that had been there a moment ago disappeared. "How could you know about that?" she asked, her expression changing.

"My kind has ways of knowing things," he said with a wry smile.

"Your kind?" she said. "Is this a pretense, or do you really believe in the vampire mythology?"

"I believe it," he said, "and you will, too." He stared into her eyes, letting his incisors slip down below his upper lip.

"Cute trick, Mr. Wymond," Dr. Dupree said, "but I hardly think that proves anything."

"Really?" he asked. "You still don't believe?" He was in front of the mirror in an instant. Her gazed remained focused on the seat he'd been in for a moment, then her eyes scanned the room until they found him. "How did you —"

"Do you see my reflection in the mirror, Dr. Dupree?" he asked. Knowing there was none, he turned to face her.

"You are a vampire," she said, smiling as recognition sparked in the violet-blue torrents of her eyes. "But...you don't want to kill me or I'd be dead already, so you must have come to play."

She rose from her seat behind the polished oak desk, moving toward him with the stealth of a feline. Her eyes held his gaze with no fear evident in them. No. What he saw there was confidence and desire. He didn't have to read her mind to know what this female was after. The scent of her pheromones grew stronger as she approached him, but he felt helpless to pull away. He felt the aura of the Sarenrea emanating from her now, along with a power he could only describe as undeniable sex appeal.

With each deliberate step, she unbuttoned a button on her suit jacket, slow and purposeful. When she'd released all three, she began undoing the buttons on her blouse, never breaking the gaze which held him in place.

But, this couldn't be. How was it that this mortal was able to have such power over him? What was happening? The only answer was that she was not just connected to the Sarenrea, but she must be witch herself. That must be it, but realizing this logic did nothing to dampen the effects. He felt anticipation rise within him, nearly as strong as when the blood lust hit him. The blood lust had replaced his sexual desires when he lost his mortality. This was highly unusual.

She undid the last button on the blouse, letting it swing open, then with a quick flick of her fingers, she released the clasp of her brazier and her voluptuous breasts were freed. The sight of her pert nipples brought his member to attention once more; another feat which should be impossible. He hadn't had a full erection in centuries, but it was standing at attention now.

At his look of surprise, she threw her head back, laughing aloud, reaching an arm out to grab his bulging bi-cep, anchoring him in place now that she'd broken her stare. Michael jerked his arm back, pulling away from her grasp, but his feet refused to move, as she reached up and grabbed the front of his navy-blue shirt, and with one quick jerk down the front of him, she ripped all the buttons from both the shirt and the suitcoat. She was mortal. Her physical strength couldn't match his, but the bond holding him was mental. Try as he might, he could not pull away from her, as her hand found his maleness through his slacks.

He let his arms fall to his sides, letting the garments slide off his arms to land on the carpet in a soft pile. It was as if all the strength had been drained from him. No, that wasn't right. It had been diverted, to the member between his legs.

His eyes found hers once more, as his member stiffened, throbbing under her touch. "How?" he asked. It was the only word he could force from his lips, as she stroked the cloth that covered his now aching cock.

For an answer, she flipped the button on his jeans open with her thumb, and before he knew it, his jeans were laying in a heap around his ankles. A moan escaped his lips as she engulfed his stiff member with her mouth. Michael hadn't felt sensual pleasure like this since he was mortal, oh so many centuries ago. Although it should be impossible, he felt the tension rising from his loins, building slow, yet it hadn't been so long that he couldn't still anticipate the urgent need for release which was sure to come.

She slid her mouth down over his cock, then pulled back her lips, scraping her teeth over the tender skin of his shaft on the way back up, making him wince. She looked up at him with those sensual violet-blues, smiling around the tip, which was still captive to her ministrations.

He strained to look over his shoulder at the mirror, which only revealed the figure of the doctor, bobbing her head up and down, her mouth forming an 'O' as she sucked air. Or at least, that was how it appeared. The feel of those full, moist lips sliding over his cock left no doubt that air wasn't what she'd wrapped her mouth around. He felt an orgasm building fast. He may not have experienced one in centuries, but he hadn't forgotten what they felt like.

She pulled back from him, sliding her hand up and down the well-oiled piston her mouth had abandoned, the pressure to cum rising with every stroke, until shot hot semen across his bare thigh. He threw his head back, abandoning what little control he had left. Dr. Dupree produced a rectangular slide, seemingly out of thin air, scraping a small amount of his semen onto it.

"What are you doing?" he said, still unable to lift his feet from the spot in front of the mirror. He watched, helpless to move, as she slid another slide over the top of the first, placing them in a small, clear plastic case.

"Just collecting a few specimens," she said, producing another slide from the medical bag, which she'd set on the floor next to him. "Sit tight now. We'll be done here in a jiff." She held up a hypodermic needle and soft rubber tubing from within the bag. She wrapped the tubing around his bi-cep, pulling it tight with her teeth. He struggled to pull his arm away, but he couldn't make it budge, even after she released the tubing. There was still some kind of mental hold on him, holding him in place.

"How is any of this possible?" he asked, demanding to know what was happening. "Let me go."

She threw her head back, laughing as she stuck her needle into his vein, withdrawing several vials of blood. "A Sarenrea witch can bring the penis of a corpse back to life. You were easy, darling."

The shock as her words sank in caused anger to rise within him. He struggled to break her hold on him, but he couldn't budge. "You are a witch! You knew!" he cried out in frustration.

"Of course, I knew," she said, as she bagged her specimens, heading for the door. "The coven said my work would raise some red flags, bringing you so I could get what I needed to complete my research. I guess they were right." She winked at him as she exited, pulling the door closed behind her.

As soon as she'd left the room, her hold was broken. Michael ran to the door, flinging it open, but she was gone. He stared out into the empty hallway, trying to get his mind around what just happened. How would he ever explain this to the Elder Council?

A True Hero

"**Y**ou're late," she said, tapping her foot on the faded linoleum.

"I know," he replied, shrugging his shoulders.

She crossed her arms and tapped her foot louder, waiting for an explanation. When it didn't come, she finally said, "Are you gonna tell me why your late?"

"Nope"

"Don't you think I deserve a reason?" she asked, raising her voice to meet the level of her anger.

"Yea, you do, but I can't give it to you," he said, so soft it was almost inaudible.

"Why not?" she demanded, lowering the volume slightly.

"You wouldn't understand," he said. "You couldn't possibly."

She stilled her tapping foot. "How do you know unless you try me?"

"I know you," he said. "You never believe anything I say."

"That's because in nineteen years, you've not once told a convincing lie," she said with a smug look. "I'll bet you were screwing off again with that Melanie chic."

"That's not it at all," he said. "That's exactly what I'm talking about. You automatically assume I'm lying, before I've even opened my mouth."

"Then what?" she said. "What is this unbelievable thing that was so important you couldn't be on time just once, on our anniversary?"

"I missed the bus and had to walk home," he said.

"I don't believe you. It's over three miles," she said, snapping at him.

"You think I don't know how far it is?" he said. "I knew you wouldn't believe me."

"Of course you do. You live in a place all your life, you must know how far it is from town," she said with a deep sigh. "So, why did you miss the bus?"

"I got caught up with something and I missed it," he said. "That's all. It happens."

"What were you doing?" she asked. Most of the wind had gone out of her sails now. She was tired. She wondered if it was even worth it.

"That's what you won't believe," he said. "I was rescuing a baby."

"Rescuing a baby?" she asked, in disbelief. In all their years together, he'd never come up with a lie so far-fetched. She didn't believe him, but she wasn't going to say it.

"Yes. Rescuing a baby," he said, nodding his head once to confirm she'd heard right.

"So... you chased a runaway stroller down a hill and grabbed it just in a nick of time, before it went out into the traffic? Or what?" she asked.

"No," he replied. "Why do you always have to be so sarcastic?"

"I'm supposed to believe that you missed the bus because you were rescuing a baby?" she said, incredulous. "You can't even save yourself." Her anger was starting to rise again. "How much have you had to drink?"

"I haven't been drinking!" he declared, shaking his head. "This is why I didn't want to tell you. See what you do?"

"All right. I'm sorry," she said, taking a deep breath and pulling herself together. She let out a long sigh. "How did you rescue a baby?"

"I helped to birth it," he said. "I saved her life."

"What?" she said, amazed by his audacity. "You have been drinking." Her foot picked up its rhythm right where it had left off. "You can't birth a baby without even being pregnant, and I say the chances of that are slim and none."

"Of course not," he said. "I didn't say I gave birth to it. I said I helped birth it."

"I don't see the difference," she said.

"Helping to birth a baby is like being in the delivery room and guiding the baby into the world."

"So, you're telling me you missed the bus because you were in a delivery room, helping to birth a baby?" she said. This was getting better and better. And he wonders why I don't ever believe him.

"I didn't say that I was in a delivery room," he said. "Just that it was like when you are in the delivery room."

"How many delivery rooms have you been in to know what it is like?" she said with a smirk.

"Very funny. Ha! Ha!" he said, raising his voice a notch.

"So, you weren't in a delivery room?" she asked, wondering why she always had to coax things out of him.

"Nope. I was in a field," he said.

"You helped birth a baby in a field?" she asked.

"Yes. That's exactly what I did," he replied.

"You see," she said, pointing a finger at him. "You can't even tell a believable lie. This is why I don't believe you."

"I am not lying!" he said, slamming his fist down on the table. "You see. I knew you wouldn't believe me."

"Well, you have to admit, it sounds pretty farfetched," she said, frustrated with him. "How am I supposed to believe something like that?"

"If you knew the whole story, you'd see," he said.

"Well then, tell me the whole story!" she almost screamed at him, stomping her foot.

"I'm trying, if you'll just shut up and listen!" he said, throwing up his hands.

"Okay, what was a pregnant mother doing in a field?" she asked. Suddenly she was not just tired, but exhausted. She didn't have the energy to argue.

"Giving birth," he said, resuming his smug attitude.

"In a field?"

"Yes, in a field," he said. "They don't take cows at the hospital."

"I hope you didn't call her a cow to her face," she said.

"No," he said. "She really was a cow."

"Pregnant women can't help but be fat," she said. "There you go being Mr. Sensitivity again."

"No. No," he said, shaking his head. "This wasn't a pregnant woman."

"Then how did she give birth?" She was getting tired of the run-around, too.

"She was a cow!" he said, nearly jumping up and down to bring his point home. She gave birth in the field because she was a real cow!"

"So, the baby you rescued..."

"Was a calf. A baby cow," he said, nodding his head enthusiastically.

"Why didn't you just say that in the first place?" she said with a sigh. She felt the first stirrings of a migraine coming on.

"So, you believe me?"

"No, but I'm trying," she said. "So, what did you do?"

"The cow was struggling," he said, beaming with pride. "I guided the calf out."

"You?" she said, tilting her head toward him. She didn't know if she believed him, but he had her interest.

"Yes, me," he replied. "I just grabbed a hold of the feet and gave her a little tug. She slid right out once the head was clear."

"It's not the sort of thing that happens every day, you know," she said.

"Yep. I'm aware of that," he said. Then he paused, looking at her. "You don't believe me, do you?"

She thought about it a moment. "Actually, I do," she said. "No one makes up a story like that. Who would believe it?"

"Obviously, you don't," he said, crossing his arms in front of him and sticking out his bottom lip in that annoying baby pout he made when he was being stubborn. She hated that pout.

"I just said that I did, didn't I?" she said, feeling annoyed with him again. "How did you know what to do?"

"I learned from Billy Crystal," he said.

"You don't even know Billy Crystal."

"I don't have to know him to learn from him," he said. "He delivered Norman on *City Slickers*."

"Who is Norman?" she asked. She knew he was baiting her, but she was determined now to see this through, hear the whole explanation, no matter how long she had to banter with him to do it.

"A baby cow, silly. Billy got to keep him at the end," he replied. "He couldn't let his calf be sold for butchering, so he took the calf home with him."

"That's television," she said. "People don't do things like that in real life."

"I do, and I can prove it," he said.

"How?" she asked.

"Bella."

"Bella?" she said. "Who is Bella?"

"My calf. Do you want to see her?"

"Wait!" she said, holding up a hand and shaking her head. She couldn't believe what she was hearing. "You brought a calf home?"

"Yep. Just like Billy Crystal," he said, grinning from ear to ear.

"That was a movie!" she said, her voice rising once more. "You can't just bring a newborn calf home. They need their mothers."

"I know that. I'm not stupid," he said. "That's why I brought Bossie along, too."

"Okay. Just hold on a minute," she said, still holding up the hand like a traffic cop, letting the cars from the other direction have a turn. "You're telling me that you brought home the cow and the calf?"

"Yep." He nodded his head, then stood silent, waiting for her response.

"Don't you think they might belong to somebody?" she asked. It was all she could think to say.

"Probably, but what else could I do?" he said. "The owner sure wasn't out in that field with me and Bossie. I couldn't just leave them there."

"You could have. Cows were giving birth and raising their calves a long time before we humans came on the scene," she said. "What are we going to do with a cow and calf?"

"Love them," he said with a shrug. "Put an ad in the paper to find the owner."

"Cows wouldn't seem to be the most loving of animals," she said, trying to imagine what they would do with a cow and a calf. Where could they even put them?

"Well, neither are you, but I'm still here," he replied with a little half-smile to show he was joking.

"Okay. Okay," she said, resigning herself to the idea, at least until they could locate their owner. "Let's go see Bossie and Bella. Where did you get those names?"

Man of Her Dreams

Disoriented, Aaron looks around taking in her surroundings. The details of last night are fuzzy. She finds herself in a doorway of paned glass, framed by red brickwork to either side. The light breeze carries unpleasant odors as she sits up, peeking around the corner of her brick cubby to find she is in an alley. It is a typical alley, with trashcans scattered up and down both sides, garbage spilling over the top of many of them. A cat comes up over the lip of one of the dumpsters two doorways down, sending a tin can spinning as it hits the ground with a metallic clang. *How did I get here?*

As her head begins to clear, she recalls the party she'd been at the previous night. She'd met a man fitting every criterion on her list for her most desirable man: tall, at least 6'3"; dark olive complexion; hair the color of midnight, slicked back into a small ponytail which curled at the base of his muscular neck and shoulders. His attire was foreign to her, way beyond the means of any of the guys she hung out with, but she had to admit he was quite attractive in a black pinstriped Armani suit, accented with bright red handkerchief, folded and tucked into his breast pocket so that one corner peeked over the top, like a kitten playing peek-a-boo. But the finishing touch was the black, floor length cape with a red silk lining, which he wore, adding to the air of mystery radiating from him. She'd wanted him. She might have left the party with him, but her memories are clouded, so she can't be sure.

She gets to her feet, standing on wobbly legs, leaning against the rough brick wall until she feels steady enough to walk. Her head pounds in the blinding noonday sun. She's always been a party animal, but she'd never been so wasted that she blacked out before. And this hangover is a killer, trying hard to bring her back to her knees. *What the hell happened last night?*

Aaron messages her stiff neck as she inches her way down the alley. The fingers of her right hand find moisture, which she tries to brush away. Glancing down at her hand, she sees smears of scarlet across her fingertips. A vision of the handsome stranger kissing her neck flashes through her memory, reawakening pleasant tingling sensations up and down her spine at the vivid image forming in her mind.

She emerges onto the deserted sidewalk. Catching a glimpse of her reflection in a shop window, she does a double take. She brushes her fingertips over her face. *What is wrong with me?* Her skin is so pale, she might be mistaken for a ghost or spirit, perhaps the walking dead. Her facial features have no color to them at all. She makes a feeble attempt to flatten down the tangled mass of auburn hair. But, there isn't much she can do. It sticks up in every direction with tangled masses protruding all over her head.

Another flash of memory strikes as she stares at her own pale image. She recalls climbing into a limousine, the feel of the real leather upholstery, smooth on the backs of her nyloned legs. Aaron glances down to see she still wears the short black cocktail dress she'd worn last night, although now it looks as if someone has shredded it with a knife, making long slits down its entire, brief length. *Why can't I remember?*

She examines her reflection in the window glass, trying to see where the blood had come from. She sees two small spots where blood is beginning to crust over on her throat. She spits on her palm, trying to rub the blood off, but only manages to swipe a bright red smudge across her neck.

She recalls necking in the back of the limo, the passion rising. They had been all over each other, groping with lustful abandon. The hand he'd slid between her legs was working her to a feverish pitch. But, along with the pleasure, there'd also been a sharp pain, where her handsome stranger had sunk his teeth into her throat, just as the hand between her legs managed to bring her over the top. Her cries had been filled with both passion and pain.

As her mind begins to clear, she recalls the feeling of panic as she tried to push him away, when she realized something wasn't right. But, it was no use. His grip on her was like a vise, his weight on her chest crushing her. Then, a feeling of light headedness as she slipped from consciousness beneath him.

That same lightheaded feeling comes over her once more at the memory. Aaron leans up against the store window until her head clears. Gathering her senses, she presses on down the sidewalk, not knowing where she is going, but needing to stay on the move, wandering, as the memories of the previous night accost her.

Her memories become clearer as each fall into place. The pieces to the puzzle begin to add up. The sensuous stranger, the ride in the limo, making out hot and heavy, how she had lost control of the situation before she'd known what was happening, making her cum through her panties. The puncture marks on her throat, (she is sure now that is what they are), offer proof that her memories are real. She'd been violated, in a manner perhaps even more intimate than had she been sexually accosted. The thought should horrify her, she knows, but every time she thinks about it she becomes aroused instead, reliving the wonderful sensations of the previous night.

A car horn blares and tires screech, bringing her back to the reality of her surroundings. She looks up to see a blue Sedan skid to a halt a few feet away from her. Aaron mouths "Sorry" to the driver, who responds by yelling out his window for her to watch where she's going, as he accelerates past her. She continues on, thinking about her coloring, wondering if this is how a person looks when all the blood has been drained from them.

Aaron wanders the streets, unaware of where her feet carry her, as the conclusion of all the facts begins to form a final picture. She looks like the walking dead, because that is what she is. Well, maybe not exactly, but she is pretty sure she'd died the previous night. The only reason she is walking now is because her mysterious stranger left her with the gift of his own blood, bonding her to him, making her one of his kind for eternity.

Where is he now? Surely, he wouldn't give his gift, only to disappear from her life forever. Forever sounded like a very long time. Just when she thought she'd found the man of her dreams. *Now what am I supposed to do?*

Stumbling through an alley on still shaky legs, she comes upon a little tan mutt digging through the spilt garbage can behind one of the many restaurants. Not so long ago, Aaron had been just like that little dog, hungry and homeless. She lucked out, getting a job as a valet in one of the downtown parking garages. She'd been able to turn her life around.

It would be just her luck. She finds the man of her dreams, is put in a position to spend all of eternity with him, and he skips out on her. Her luck with men had never been good, but for him to abandon her after he had gotten what he wanted from her, changing her existence for eternity, was the worst insult anyone of the male persuasion had ever perpetrated upon her. He's given her the chance to start over, perhaps hold the world at her fingertips, but without his guidance, she'd probably screw it up just like she did everything else in her life. At the thought of this, anger bubbles within her, surprising her with a rumbling growl deep down in her throat, coaxing a startled yelp from the mutt. She watches in puzzlement as he runs off down the alley, tail tucked.

Aaron sniffs the air around her, catching the coppery odor of something she can't quite put a finger on which stirs hunger pangs deep within her, deeper, more severe than anything she's experienced before. Her nostrils twitch, flaring as she walks with purpose, unable to prevent her feet from moving forward, as if of their own accord, as the scent assails her, pulling her forward.

Turning a corner, she collides with a woman who'd been coming from the other direction. The impact knocks the papers the woman had been carrying out of her hands, scattering them across the cement of the sidewalk. The scent is overwhelming. Aaron mumbles an apology, scooping up papers the wind is trying to carry away, handing them back to the woman, brushing her fingertips with her own.

As they make contact, it becomes apparent this woman was the source of the scent Aaron has been following, a deep scent lying beneath the smell of the woman's perfume, which strikes a sense of revulsion within her. Yet... her eyes are drawn to the bluish vein throbbing along the woman's throat, rising near the surface of her supple skin. Before she realizes what she's doing, she springs, sinking her teeth into the woman's throat, drinking from the fountain of life fluid flowing within with greed and abandon.

Wiping her lips in satisfaction, she pulls back from the corpse which now lies in her arms. She drops the lifeless body on the sidewalk littered with the woman's papers, setting out with new purpose. Her little 'snack' has rejuvenated her. The realization she's become what she'd feared, brings with it a new feeling of strength. Her thoughts are crystal clear. This is indeed a new start, and Aaron plans to take full advantage of the opportunity.

A smile forms on Aaron's face, her eyes sparking with her new sharper, clearer vision. Her world is now filled with possibilities, but she won't make this new start alone. The man of her dreams will not get away from her. She has a whole eternity to spend looking for him and she possesses the ability to hunt him down. Licking the last drops of blood from her lips with satisfaction, she strides away with a new confidence, an invigorating energy.

The more she thinks about the man of her dreams, the more obsessed she becomes with the idea of finding him. She'll start at the party location. The hunted and hunter are about to switch places.

AARON PICKS UP HIS scent co-mingled with the scents of others outside the party house, on the curb where they had waited for the car to be brought around by the valet, but it disappears there. She doesn't know how she knows it is his scent, but she does. It's a musky, sensual smell. She sniffs the air, trying to pick it up again, but it is no use. When he'd gotten into the car, his scent had gone with him, of course. *There are no valets now, during the heat of the day. No, this is a night place.*

She steps forward, rapping on the plate glass door of the two-story mansion before her. She catches her reflection in the glass of the door as she waits for someone to answer. Her color has improved, which doesn't surprise her, because she feels great. She feels strong, rejuvenated, renewed. She takes in her cheeks, which are now flushed with a rosy hue, and noticed the inhuman reddish gleam cast by her eyes. *That's because I'm not human any more... And because I fed.*

A short, balding man answers the door in a pair of dripping navy blue swim trunks. "Can I help you?" he asks, looking her up and down, reminding her of her disheveled state, which she hadn't thought to do anything about.

"Hello," she says, knowing it is too late to make a good first impression. "I was here, at your party last night."

"Yeah, so?" he says with a questioning look, a puddle forming beneath him on the tiles of the entry. "There were a lot of people here last night. What do you want?"

"I met a man here," she says, trying to look innocent. "I left with him, but after he dropped me off, I realized I'd left the card he'd given me in his car. I thought maybe you would know who he is."

"Like I said, lady, there were a lot of people here last night," he says, pushing the door closed.

"If you didn't see us, maybe someone else inside did," Aaron says, throwing out her arm to prevent him from closing the door on her. To her surprise, the door flies open, knocking the man backwards into the entryway, his head slamming against the wall. He crumples to the floor in a wet heap. She hesitates for a moment, shocked by her newly acquired strength. Then she continues on, stepping over the unconscious man as she picks up the scent of her mystery man once more.

Aaron marches through the entry and down the hall leading into the kitchen, where two women are busy preparing food and chattering with one another. They might have been sisters, if not for the age difference. One woman is young, perhaps in her twenties or early thirties, with long dark hair. The other woman is older, her dark hair graying at the temples, but they share the same sharp facial features. *Perhaps mother and daughter then.* They both wear gray maid's uniforms with white aprons.

Aaron snaps her fingers above her head to get their attention. "Ladies, listen up," she says. "I'm looking for a man who I met here last night. He's very tall and handsome. He was wearing a long black cape. Ring any bells?" she asks.

The older woman shakes her head with vigor in denial. The younger woman hesitates, then follows the older woman's example.

Aaron steps in front of the younger one. "Something you're not telling me?" she says, looking the woman in the eye. "I got the feeling he felt at home here, as if he were a frequent guest."

The young woman trembles, her lower lip quivering. *Why is she so scared?* Aaron looks down at her shredded skirt and ripped stockings. *No wonder she's afraid.* "Hey, don't be afraid," she says, softening her voice. "Please, I must find this man. My future may depend on it. Do you know him?"

The younger woman's eyes shift, glancing at the older woman. Then she turns, giving a nod. The older woman gives a tiny shake of her head, but the younger woman proceeds anyway. "H-he's the master of the house, the host of the party. You don't know this?"

Aaron's eyes narrow as she questions the woman. "He lives here?"

"I saw you leave with him," she says, nodding her head once more. Then, she looks into Aaron's eyes, her own eyes pleading. "Please, don't tell him I told you. I have a little girl to raise."

"Where can I find him?" Aaron asks. "Is he here now?"

The younger woman opens her mouth to speak, looking down the hallway to the stair case. "He's…"

"Anita, no!" the older woman cries with a gasp, cutting off her words.

Anita hesitates once more, then shakes her head. "I'm sorry. I can say no more. I need this job."

Aaron turns toward the stairs, where she catches that musky scent once more. "Don't worry, I can find him," she says, calling back over her shoulder as she moves down the hallway and begins to climb, sniffing the whole way. "He'll never know we spoke."

She is learning her new abilities are pretty cool. She, who got winded going up a slight incline, now bounds up the flight of stairs, two at a time, without even breathing hard. She inhales deep as she enters the second-floor hallway, filling her lungs just to prove that she can. She takes long, confident strides down the hallway toward the door at the end, which is ajar, allowing a small sliver of light to spill out onto the rose pattern of the carpet. She doesn't stop when she reaches it, but shoves it open with her arm, charging in unannounced.

He is sitting behind a heavy oak desk. He raises his head to look up at her as she enters, a mildly startled expression crossing over his face. "Well, I can't say I was expecting to see you again," he says. "How in the hell did you find me?"

Aaron leaps up onto the desk which separates them. She gazes down at him with a sly smile on her face, running her tongue over her lips. "Your smell is strong," she says. "My new nose trailed you with ease."

He leans back in his chair, tilting it to look up at her, an approving look dawning on his face. "The way you've already mastered some of your gifts, it seems you're pretty comfortable with them. That entrance indicates you may even be enjoying them," he says. "So, if you're not angry with me, then why are you here? What do you want?"

She glares down at him, but she knows he isn't scared of her. "I want you," she says, pointing her finger at his chest. "Why would you share your gift, then just... leave me there on the street all alone?" She stomps her foot on the desk to emphasize the last syllables. "You think you can just drink and run? That's a hell of a way to treat a girl."

Recognition dawns in his eyes. "Ah, I see," he says, pointing from himself to her. "You think because I chose you last night, there should now be something between us?"

"Well... yes," she says, stammering at his unexpected question. "When you share something as intimate as we did, it seems there must be more. You've given me a chance to start over, but I don't want to embark on this wonderful new existence alone. You're everything I've ever wanted in a man."

"Ah... but I'm not a man," he replies, holding a finger up, giving her a knowing look.

"True," she says, considering his comment. "But, in that same regard, I'm no longer a woman either."

There is an uncomfortable silence between them as each considers the situation, trying to imagine what should come next.

"So, let me guess," he says, folding his arms behind his head, placing his feet up on his desk. "You think you should just hang out with me for the rest of eternity?"

"No... er, well, yes," she says. When he puts it that way, it does seem like she is demanding a bit much of him. "I mean, ah... it's obvious what you did isn't like when humans take a mate. But, don't you have at least some obligation... to like, make sure I have a good start in this new existence?"

"No, it's not like when humans bring offspring into the world either," he says, shaking his head. "I'm afraid you're not my child, or my lover."

"How about a companion, then?" she asks, giving him her sweetest smile, turning on the charm to hide the panic she felt inside. He can't leave her to her own devices. It is his fault she's in this condition. She doesn't have a back-up plan in the event this confrontation fails. "Don't you ever get lonely?"

He puts his head back, leaning even further back in his chair, letting out a belly laugh, loud and guttural. "Yes. At times I do get lonely. But when I do, I chose someone to imbibe with... for a short time."

"So, that's all I am to you?" she asks, feeling her anger rising from her gut once more. "A one night stand?" She leaps from the desk, pouncing like a cat, landing on top of him, her knees resting on the arms of the chair. With him reclined as he is, she's pinned him. She's in control, holding her outrage in check. She bores into him with her eyes. "How can you be so callous?"

She lowers her head to sink her teeth into his neck, but before she knows what is happening, he pushes her off with surprising force. She flies backwards, smashing into a filing cabinet in the corner across the room before sliding down to the carpet.

"Do you think your new abilities are enough to overpower me?" he says in a voice that's more of a roar, as he rises to his feet. Crossing the room in an instant, he towers above her as she looks up at him.

"Wow! You really know how to reject a girl," she says, fighting the urge to cower before his overbearing presence, unwilling to let him see the fright he's stirred within her. She forces herself to get up from the floor, facing him. "Nothing like letting me down easy."

"Out of all the hundreds of years I've roamed this earth. All of the playmates I've chosen during that time, I've never had one come looking for me. I've never justified my actions to anyone!" His roaring voice is deafening.

Aaron rises to her feet, shaking her head to get her thoughts straight. The unexpected flight across the room rattled her, but her head seems to be clearing. She isn't about to cow down to him just because he can muster some volume. She straightens her back, smoothing her torn skirt as best she can. "Well, now you've had one come looking," she says, meeting his gaze and surpassing him in decibels. "What are you going to do about it?!"

He looks her over as she squares herself in front of him. "You do have some spunk," he says with a shrug of his shoulders and a low chuckle. "That's why I chose you." He takes a step forward, reaching out, placing a finger under her chin, raising it up. She meets his gaze as he examines her features. "That, and the fact you are very beautiful, indeed. Maybe we could... work something out, if you still want to be my companion."

His change in attitude catches her by surprise. She searches the depths of his eyes, but there is no way to know if he is sincere. There could be another outburst of rage lying just below the surface, ready to erupt. She came there wanting what he is now offering. She wanted to learn, to understand what it is she has become. Now, she isn't so sure. Maybe she doesn't know what she wants, or maybe she just doesn't trust him. "Why?" she demands, stepping back away from his touch. "Why would you do this when you never have before? Why for me?"

"Because you are beautiful. Because there is fire in your eyes," he says, relaxing his posture. "Because you're not afraid of me, even though you should be. There aren't many who would stand up to me the way you just did."

"So, you're serious?" she asks, still suspicious of him. "Now, you want me to stay here with you?"

"I don't know if I'm talking about for eternity or anything," he says, shrugging his shoulders. "But I think we could make it work for a while." He gives her a wink.

Aaron lets a smile cross over her face as she allows herself to believe his offer might be genuine. "You'll teach me?"

"Yes. I'll help you to develop your new talents and abilities," he says with a sigh. "I'm sure we can come to terms which are agreeable to both of us. You seem to be a quick study."

"What do I have to do?" she asks, still skeptical. "What do you get out of the deal?"

"I get the pleasure of your company," he says, stepping toward her, sliding an arm around her waist. "Like you said, being a vampire can be pretty lonely. You were a lot of fun last night and up to now, you've been full of surprises."

"Not good enough," she says, placing a hand on his chest to hold him off. "I want to be more than just a plaything who entertains you. When I left with you last night, we had a spark. I thought you were the man of my dreams."

"We've already determined I'm not a man at all, so that is an impossibility, but I could get used to having you around. Can we start over? Maybe we could make some new dreams together?" he says, pulling her close to him. He nuzzles his face into the crook of her neck, whispering into her ear. "To me, it sounds better than seeing who can bash the other senseless. I think that's what it must come to otherwise. What do you say?"

"I don't even know your name," she says, looking up at him with a shy smile, happier than she'd ever been in life. It doesn't matter he isn't a man. She's found the vampire of her dreams, and he is hers, maybe not for eternity, but at least for now. Starting over might be fun.

A Woman's World

"My sisters in strife, I come before you today in celebration," Queen Oprah says. Applause rises and she waits for them to quiet before continuing. "For today we have finally accomplished our goals of banning disgusting men to the dregs of society where they belong. As of today, we have banished men from all positions of power and authority, confining them to the tasks of menial labor that they were created to do."

The crowd of women rises to their feet clapping and cheering loud and long. "From today forward," Queen Oprah continues when the crowd quiets once more, "we will never have to feel a man's touch on the sacredness of the holy vessels that are our bodies again. Men have been put in their place, and from today forward it is a woman's world!"

She raises her fist in triumph and the crowd of women go berserk, stomping their feet, clapping their hands, crying out her name, "Queen Oprah! Queen Oprah!"

Queen Oprah! Bah! The sound of it makes me want to puke. I pull back from the hole in the fence which I've been watching through, mentally urging my stomach to settle. Even when I'm not watching, the plank fence that stands between me and the stage on the other side isn't thick enough to drown out the sound of the cheering, and I have to see. So, I put my eye back against the plank with the hole and look out over a stadium filled to overflowing with women, all women, not a man to be seen. I am still trying to get my mind around the fact that this thing has really happened. Almost overnight, I've become a member of a minority group, and not just any minority group – men are now the lepers of the twenty-first century, shunned and isolated. Last week, I had a family, a wife and son, and now here I am, watching my wife, Carolynn, kiss ass to the woman whose movement has castrated an entire nation.

A finger taps my shoulder and I turn around to find a stranger standing behind me. He appears to be in his fifties, with short cropped white hair, and neatly trimmed facial hair of the same color. He wears a wrinkled short sleeve button up shirt, a black tie hanging loose around his neck and a suit jacket slung over his shoulder. He looks worn and frazzled. "Pardon me sir," the man says, pleading with his eyes for understanding. "Could you tell me what the hell is going on around here?"

"What do you mean?" I ask, puzzled that anyone can be that clueless. The whole world has witnessed the symbolic castration of the former President for his alleged sins against those of the female persuasion. Every corner of the Earth is aware of the rapid rise to power made by Oprah, as women picked the government and media apart, ridding both arenas of all males. How can this guy not know what has been happening in this country? I put a finger to my lips, to quiet him, lest he draw unwanted attention to us. "You certainly know how to startle a person," I say in a hushed voice.

"I've been out of the country for several months," he says, placing a hand above his eyes to block the glare of the sun. "When I left, we had a President, although not a very popular one, but now it seems we have a Queen?"

"That's what she wants to be called, yes. Take a look," I say, stepping back so he can step up to the hole in the fence. I can't tolerate the idea of Oprah as Queen, but I don't know this lad. Best to watch my tongue and let him draw his own conclusions. "She claimed the term President had too many masculine implications and was too political sounding. Apparently, royalty had a better ring to her."

"That's Oprah Winfrey, the talk show hostess and television personality. But how did this happen?" he asks. "Where are all the men? How is this possible? It's not even an election year."

"Where have you been, man," I ask, "that you don't know about the modern-day witch hunt that has gone on here? Women have persecuted us, just as the accused witches were persecuted during the inquisition. Once accused of sexually inappropriate behavior, guilt or innocence matters not, for your life is over. You lose all you ever had, family, career, status... Hell, the President of the United States was castrated, first by the media and then by their new female driven courts after Oprah took her throne. I hear they plan to do an actual physical castration right here today to make a public example of him. How can you not know?"

"That's awful," he says, scrunching up his nose as if he'd smelled something bad. "I'm a scientist. I've been in North Korea. I was invited there, secretly of course, to observe their nuclear program, but I'm not a traitor." He holds up a hand as if to curb an unspoken accusation. "The President commissioned me to go to gather information, but he didn't want it to be publicly known. It was a matter of national security. The only news allowed there is that put out by the North Korean government. Although there was plenty of propaganda against the U.S., mostly directed at the President, I saw little else pertaining to home. I knew something was up when they ushered me out of the country with no explanation and shipped me back home. I guess I was lucky to be away when this witch hunt took place, huh?"

"I don't know about that," I say, taking another peek through the hole. It's best to keep an eye on the happenings, even if they turn my stomach. I don't want to be caught by surprise. "It seems to me you're still in a pickle. You just don't realize it."

"How do you figure?" he asks. "They can't do anything to me. I've done nothing inappropriate. I haven't even been in the states for the past year."

"Don't be too sure," I say. He really doesn't understand the situation. I suppose I have some obligation to try and make him see. "It's not just forcing women to have sex or uninvited groping. Many men are paying the price for making a pass at a woman at a time when that's just what men did. Making a pass was once a common social behavior. Now it's been decided that making passes at women is unacceptable, and every man who ever made one must pay, even if it was made during times when it was considered acceptable behavior. They can say you did something thirty years ago. Nobody's safe, I tell you."

"If what you say is true," he says, scratching his chin as he sorts it all out, "then I have no home left to go to. What will I do?"

"None of us have a home to go to anymore," I say. I take another look through the hole. Not much has changed. Queen Oprah speaks and the stadium full of women cheer her blindly. She could describe her morning bowel movement and they would still cheer. "They're using our muscle to build labor camps outside the cities, where the men will all be housed and used to operate their industries. The only exceptions are those who have special talents and abilities that they have a need for, and the alternative genders, who they allow to function as personal servants and assistants. I guess women don't feel threatened by those guys. All other men are fair game."

"So, who are you?" he asks. "How is it that you are out here instead of being persecuted with the others? What makes you special?"

"I'm nobody special," I say with a shrug. "I'm just a lowly stock broker, but my wife is one of Queen Oprah's inner circle. I overheard a phone conversation and I hid when they came to get me. I was just lucky, that's all."

He leans forward and takes another peek through the hole. "Do you think my expertise in nuclear warfare would be a benefit to them?" he asks.

I turn and stare at him, trying to figure out if he's serious or not. It is incredulous to think that he might be. These women have destroyed all that America stands for. "If you weren't a traitor by going over to North Korea, you will be now," I say.

"It wouldn't be the first time I've sold out to the highest bidder. We all do what we have to do to survive. I could put on a dress and say I identify as female. Then, they'll talk to me," the man says, turning to head toward the entrance to the stadium. "We should be able to get this cleared up soon."

"It won't work, I tell you," I say, grabbing him by the arm and pulling him back. "They can sniff out the phonies. "Somehow, they'll know if you're the real deal. If they catch you, that's treason and the penalty is death."

"They can't get away with that," he says, jerking his arm back. "This is America! We all have rights."

"Listen to that," I say, pointing a thumb at the fence to indicate the sound of applause and cheering coming from the other side. "You can't argue with that. There's no winning. There are no rights anymore. It's a woman's world now."

"That's ridiculous," he says. "What will they do without men?"

"Apparently, anything they want," I reply. "Women have long since stopped needing us to provide for them, or protect them."

"I mean, how will they be fruitful and multiply?" he asks. "How can they reproduce? They need men for that."

"You really are uninformed," I say. I am starting to feel annoyed. Can't this guy figure anything out for himself? "Modern technology? Artificial insemination? Cloning? Ring any bells?"

"This isn't right," he says, looking a bit forlorn. "They can't eliminate our entire gender. What about the men who haven't been offensive in any way?"

"Doesn't matter," I say with a shrug of my shoulders. "All it takes is one accusation and they come out of the woodwork in droves."

"Wh-what am I going to do?" he asks, now looking downright lost. "I can't survive in a labor camp. I'm not cut out to be a slave doing manual labor. We have to get out of the country before it's too late." With that, he grows quiet. I imagine he's beginning to process all that he's learned. He must be having the same realization I did when I watched Oprah make her speech at the Golden Globes, launching her *Time's Up* campaign – as men, we're screwed.

"It's already too late," I say, verbalizing the dread I've had for the last few days. I'm not sure why I'm considering sharing my plan with this stranger, but I'm mulling over the idea. Maybe because I feel we have something in common. We are kindred spirits, as Carolynn would say. The thought of my wife's betrayal is enough to strengthen my commitment to my plan, but I'm not ready to spill the beans just yet. "It's useless to try to stow away on a ship. They've tightened security on all of the ports," I say. "And they've accelerated the construction of Trump's wall on the southern border to keep us in."

"Oprah won't have any better luck than any of the leaders before her in stopping illegal immigration," he says, pulling his arm back. "How can she think she'll be successful where so many have failed?"

"No, they aren't trying to keep people out. Women are flooding in here from all countries, especially those in the Middle East," I explain. "Their security measures are to keep the men from escaping. If they let us all go, they'd be without a workforce."

His eyes grow wide and I see real fear there for the first time. "Then, what are we going to do?" he asks. "There's no way out, if what you say is true."

"No, but I have a plan," I say, reaching inside my jacket to be sure the gun is still there. I've decided to share my secret with this man. Really there is no one else for me to share it with. But before I can say more the crowd goes wild on the other side of the fence. "Wait, there's something going on."

I step back up to the hole in the fence and take another peek. They are dragging a man who looks strangely familiar out onto the stage kicking and screaming in a most undignified manner. Two large men lift him by his arms and carry him, so his efforts to resist are fruitless. They are dressed as women, but their size and the tattoos on their muscular biceps give away their natural maleness.

"You're fired!" Trump screams. "I'm the President of the United States! You're all fired!"

"Not any more", Queen Oprah says, strutting across the stage in front of him. "When we're done with you, you won't even be a man."

"What's going on?" the scientist asks, tapping me on the shoulder.

I glance back over my shoulder and then sidestep to make room for him to peer through the hole. When he pulls back, all the color has drained from his face. I regain my spot in front of the hole.

"You can't do this to me, you don't have the..." Trump is cut off as Queen Oprah walks over and stuffs a cloth in his mouth.

"You're right. I don't have the right to do anything to you. Let me introduce you to your accusers." She turns to the audience and projects her voice over the crowds. "Ladies! I give you Ivanna Trump!"

There is applause and cheers as Ivanna comes out onto the stage. As it dies down a little Queen Oprah pinches Trumps chin between her fingers, forcing him to look out upon the crowd. "Perhaps you remember the first wife you cheated on?" Then she turns to the crowd, but she still addresses Trump. "Or Marla Maples, the mistress you dumped by the wayside as soon as someone better came along?" Miss Maples strolls onto the stage to more cheers and applause. "Or maybe your porn star fling, Stephanie Clifford?"

Miss Clifford enters the stage and stands with the other women, who are lined up to face Trump.

"We've found nineteen women who accuse you of sexual harassment, as well."

Trump shakes his head violently, his eyes nearly popping out of his head, his face beat red as the line of women parade across the stage. Growling noises issue from him, the most he can do with a rag in his mouth.

"Last but not least," Queen Oprah continues, "I'm sure you remember your lovely wife, Melania."

I draw in breath as Melania appears on stage, prodded forward by my own wife, Carolynn. There are tears streaming down Melania's cheeks, making black trails over her beautiful face. Carolynn's face looks hard as stone.

Trump goes crazy when he sees his wife. He rips one arm away from his captor's grasp and lunges toward his wife. The goon immediately jerks him back into place, of course, but not before I see the pain in his eyes. He may be uncouth. He may be a political disaster. But no man deserves to be publicly castrated in front of the woman he loves.

Forced to stand on the stage with the other women who have come forward to condemn him, Melania cries, "I won't do it, Don. I won't do what they ask. I love you."

"Oh, a male sympathizer," Queen Oprah says. "If you aren't with us, then you're against us. Guards! Seize her!"

The two guards holding Trump let go of him and go after Melania. Trump rips the rag out of his mouth and lunges for them, screaming, "Nooooo!"

Oprah yells at the guards, "You buffoons!"

I see my chance and pull the gun from the shoulder holster under my jacket, placing the muzzle against the hole in the fence. I have Oprah in my sites, preparing to pull the trigger, when the scientist yells, "He's got a gun! He's going to assassinate the Queen!"

Carolynn lunges at Oprah, knocking her out of the line of fire just as I squeeze the trigger and Carolynn takes my bullet instead. Then, several women pounce on me, knocking me to the ground. I look up to see two more women, slamming the scientist into the fence. "No, not me! He tried to assassinate the Queen, not me!"

I realize I was right all along. It's a woman's world and we're screwed.

If you like a story, be sure to leave a review.
It's okay to post a review that's only about the stories you read.

Thank you for reading

Last Call

and other short fiction

by

Kaye Lynne Booth

Did you love *Last Call and Other Short Fiction*? Then you should read *Ask the Authors*[1] by Kaye Lynne Booth et al.!

The author reference every budding author should have. Writing tips and advice from 17 experienced authors who are published in varied genres. Each author shares why they write and what inspires them with an inside glimpse into their individual writing processes. Learn what works for them and what doesn't in crafting a good story, editing and revision, publishing, the business end of writing, and marketing and promotion.

---

1. https://books2read.com/u/mdzvwO

2. https://books2read.com/u/mdzvwO

About the Author

Kaye Lynne Booth lives, works and plays in the mountains of Colorado. With a dual emphasis M.F.A. in Creative Writing, writing is more than a passion. It's a way of life. She's a multi-genre author, who finds inspiration from the nature around her, and her love of the old west, and other odd and quirky things which might surprise you. She has short stories featured in the following anthologies: *The Collapsar Directive* ("If You're Happy and You Know It"); *Relationship Add Vice* ("The Devil Made Her Do It"); *Nightmareland* ("The Haunting in Carol's Woods"); *Whispers of the Past* ("The Woman in the Water"); and Spirits of the West. Her western, *Delilah,* and her author's reference, *Ask the Authors* are also available now.

In her spare time, she keeps up her author's blog, *Writing to be Read,* where she posts reflections on her own writing, author interviews and book reviews, along with writing tips and inspirational posts from fellow writers. She's also the founder of *WordCrafter.* In addition to creating her own imprint in *WordCrafter Press,* she offers quality author services, such as editing, social media & book promotion, and online writing courses through *WordCrafter Quality Writing & Author Services.* When not writing or editing, she is bird watching, or hiking, or just soaking up some of that Colorado sunshine.

Read more at https://kayebooth.wixsite.com/wordcrafter.